RAW CANVAS

Books by Ian Bloom

SCREWDRIVER
SAVAGE RECREATION
RAW CANVAS

Raw Canvas

Ian Bloom

LIBRARY OF CONGRESS CATALOGING-IN-
PUBLICATION DATA
Bloom, Ian, 1990-Present.
Raw Canvas/Ian Bloom
ISBN 978-1-944527-02-0

Printed in the United States of America

9 9 9 6 1 8

IAN BLOOM

Ian Bloom is an American artist born on February 15, 1990. Working in concert with collectors, Bloom markets abstract and realistic paintings, alongside photographs, drawings, films, music, fashion, and literature. Bloom was born on Sunset Boulevard in Hollywood, Los Angeles, California, the only child of an interracial marriage. His mother, Akiko, from Japan, worked for a prominent Japanese bank, and his father, Barry, an American, is a renowned cardiac anesthesiologist. They met in Mexico during graduate school, later moving to Washington, D.C., then New York, and finally Los Angeles. His Ashkenazi Jewish great-grandparents immigrated from Russia, Poland, and Germany; his grandparents and his father were born in New York. Growing up off of Mulholland Drive in Los Angeles, Bloom spent vacations with his grandparents in the town of Miyazaki near Toyama, and alternated his time between Japan and Europe. His travels through Italy, Switzerland, France, Monaco, Spain, England, Austria, and Vatican City shaped his global perspective and artistry. At age 16, Bloom completed Art History and Film Studies courses at Columbia University, followed by Political Science and Comparative Literature courses at the University of California, Berkeley, at 17. Between 2008 and 2013, he pursued a double major in Accounting and Marketing at New York University's Stern School of Business and graduated with Bachelor's degrees in both disciplines, and a Master of Science degree in Accounting in 2013. Bloom has worked as an actor and as a Certified Public Accountant, but got his start in the art world selling his literature online. With an original vision and tactical execution, Bloom continues to expand his portfolio, driven by a relentless pursuit of excellence, innovation, and aesthetic mastery.

RAW CANVAS

Contents

1

A Baja Summer

I swung my legs out of the bed and sat there trying to remember what had happened after that last glass of tequila. I drew a blank. I got out of bed and took inventory of my effects. "Fountain pen gone. It leaked anyway. Never had one that didn't. Pocket knife gone. No loss either." I began putting on my clothes. I had the shakes bad. "Need a few quick beers. Maybe I can catch Rollins home now."

It was a long walk. Rollins was in front of his apartment, walking his Norwegian elk-hound. He was a solidly built man of my age, taller with strong, handsome features and wiry, black hair a little gray at the temples. He was wearing an expensive sports shirt, whipcord slacks, and a suede leather jacket. We had known each other our entire lives.

Rollins listened to my account, or lack of, of the previous evening. "You're going to get your head blown off carrying that gun," he said. "What do you carry it for? You wouldn't know what you were shooting at. You bumped into trees twice there outside Benito's. You walked right in front of a car. I pulled you back and then you threatened me. I left you there to find your own way home, and I don't know how you ever made it." He paused, puffed his smoke. "I tell you, everyone is fed up with the way you've been acting lately. If there's one thing I don't want to be around, and I think no one else would care to be around, it's a drunk with a gun."

"You're right, of course," I caved.

"Well, I want to help you in any way I can. But the first thing you have to do is cut down on the sauce and build up your health. You look fucking terrible. Then, you'd better think about making some money. Speaking of money, I guess you're broke, as usual." Rollins took out his wallet. "Here's fifty pesos. That's the best I can do for you."

I got drunk on the fifty pesos. About nine that night, I ran out of money and went back to my apartment. I lay down and tried to sleep. When I closed my eyes, I saw an Oriental face, the lips and nose eaten away by disease. The disease spread, melting the face into an amoeboid mass in which the eyes floated, dull crustacean eyes. Slowly, a new face formed around the eyes. A series of faces, hieroglyphs, distorted and leading to the final place where the human road ends, where the human form can no longer contain the crustacean horror that has grown inside it.

I watched curiously, eyes open shut. "I got the horrors," I thought as a matter of fact. My mind was active, and the images would not quit their hustle against my attempts to sleep, so I stayed up. Had a bottle of wine in my dresser I was saving for a special occasion but cracked it open anyway.

Before the sun rose, sleep overtook me, but I fumbled in and out, semi-aware of the weather and the discomfort of the armchair. I think it rained in waves, and by the time I conjured the will to rise up, the rain had stopped. The layer of drying water over the windowsill encouraged me to look out onto the street. The sheer black pavement looked waxed over with the sun's rays streaking zigzag. The morning smoke on a dense Sunday morning really made me upbeat, happy to be awake amidst the pretty deca-dence. I could hear the early movers' commotion on the street below, yelling over street craps, a few car tires gliding over the gravel. The entire street had been undergoing a renovation to en-courage more business. This gravel was the clearest sound of the construction.

Anyhow, I remembered I had to meet a friend at the bus station before noon, and I hastily gathered myself to enter the public arena. On the way, I glanced at the mail the concierge in the lobby had forcibly handed me. "Señor Jerry, señor Jerry, sus correos." I threw them all in a litter bin, except the one I opened from the newspaper. My assignment had been extended. And with that, an-other thousand words on a separate subject. Glad of my fortune to stay, the next week of debauchery looked good as two weeks. The bus station was crowded, I assumed for the political event set to take place at the end of the week. This comprised the extension of my assignment.

A stampede of children and brothers and sisters of the locale bombarded the area. Out of the ruckus emerged Brent Baxter. Baxter was a college buddy of mine; he had been the ace pitcher on the university team, even got All-American honorable mention a year or two. Now, he was en route to the southern coast, but saw an excuse to postpone arriving at his destination with me as way-point. He still had the athletic mold, brimming out of his three-piece.

"Briggs, you son of a gun, how are you?" We shook hands, and I told him we'd catch a drink and sandwich at the plaza by the hotel. We walked and caught up.

"Cannot complain, this place is a hell of a lotta fun, I tell you."

"Exactly what I'd like to hear. Tell me more."

"Cheap, biting tequila. The right amount of warm weather. And the women, you will just see for yourself."

"I need some sort of respite. Headed out to my cousin's wedding, as you know, really stings me to be amongst all my kin, drunk, and alone."

"Santa Rosalía will treat you righteous." He dropped off his luggage, and we sat out on the veranda of Jose's. The waitress was a pretty thing, and she was most friendly to the newcomer. Baxter really got a kick out of the warm welcome; he felt out of place amongst the Mexicalis. A few shots of tequila settled his nerves.

"Jerry, man, this town's got me hooked."

"You don't say?"

"I may have just arrived, but my gut tells me I could fit in here."

"I can tell you all the reasons why you can't fit here."

"The booze won't overtake me. Nor the women. The lawlessness south of America has me feeling adventurous."

"When's the wedding?"

"This weekend, got a few days to get acquainted here." Rollins spotted us across the street and took a seat at the veranda. He joined in on the conversation.

"Rollins, here, should be able to provide you with all the answers to your questions, Baxter."

"Well, Rollins, can we find a game, poker perhaps?"

"I know a guy with a greyhound around the way. Hosts games in an old mining facility right there, just down the block. Quite an establishment, if I say so myself." Baxter's eyes gleamed with the hope of a quick score, and his wayward gaze carried over to me. I was in. We had a few more drinks, and I was set to take a siesta to prepare for the night's risks and rewards. These Mexicalis were deceptive, they tried to intimidate with their machismo, so I had to be on guard, mainly to look out for Baxter. He was a newcomer, and they could always smell the sweat on a newcomer. Nothing really happened for a while. Baxter and I drank excessively. We shifted inside after the shade went away on the veranda. Rollins stuck around but got caught up reading the American newspaper. He had a large wager on a baseball game, and judging by his frantic movements towards the phone, it had not gone his way. I was thoroughly entertained by his plight; I think tonight, he'd be extra aggressive at the tables. Baxter started losing his wind, and I told him I'd meet him after the nap—we'd catch a coffee and meal prior to the games.

I awoke after sunset and noticed I really needed a shower. Not so much that I was covered in dirt but rather that my mind was dragging on me. This liquor binge still had legs for the time being, and my willpower would not put me out of commission just yet. Baxter was outside the lobby smoking a cigarette when I came down. He had a shit-eating grin on his face when I approached. "Got a proposition for you, Jerr. I know, you already have a bad feeling, but hear me out." I lit my own cigarette and the smoke cleared as he continued proposing. "So, I just spotted these two cool broads down at Jose's, where we were at earlier. They're just aching, and I can admit I am, too. Whaddya say we skip the tables tonight and take 'em out on the town?"

"I'm fair game, but just so you don't forget, you're the one looking for that big score, at least so I thought."

"Scores come in dresses and envelopes. And these dresses are too shiny to overlook. Let's go."

"Hope Rollins won't lose his cool tonight. That baseball game sure had him mucked up."

"Fuck, Rollins. High-nosed, self indulgent. He'll be in one piece when we see him tomorrow. But, please, onward we go, never have I seen you so unwilling to pursue prime meat, Briggs." The cigarettes were finished and we sauntered over to the veranda, now alit by flamed lamps and loud, liberated voices. People were getting drunk, and the local types really knew how to lose their inhibitions. I followed Baxter's lead, he was hungry and eager. These two ladies were positioned righteously for us, on the edge of the patio area with open tables on both sides of theirs. We made our way, and Baxter didn't have to do much. He was American.

Their names were Maria and Layla. They were full-figured and their bodies breathed underneath those dresses. Always amazed me how women always said they were cold, but when attracting men, they always seemed to wear less and less. Baxter honed in on Maria and I was left with Layla. She was prettier than Maria, I thought, and was glad to be speaking to her, drinking, smoking, and losing care in her oceanic eyes.

"Been here much?"

"Not so much."

"I'm here for work; Brent's here for pleasure."

"Funny; I thought you were here for pleasure."

"I'm a writer. Work and fun mix quite well."

"You should write about me. I'm quite the experienced lady."

"Your English is right. I'm beginning to think you're American."

"American, America, ah, no, Mr. Briggs. I've spent time abroad most of my life, España and the UK. Mi abuela is ill and I see to her here."

"That's mighty kind of you. Is it fatal?"

"No, no, she's just so lonely. Mi abuelo's been gone for a few years, and the ranch is too big just for her. She gets royal service from me."

"Well, I'm glad the pressure's off and you're relaxing in good company, now."

"You consider yourself good company?"

"With vigor. Señor! More drinks."

"Well you're headed in the right direction, always a gentleman buys the lady a drink."

"It's a healthy excuse for you to be interested." She smirked, holding back a friendly smile and looked away, lighting a cigarette. She crossed her legs tighter and adjusted her dress as she shifted left. In the veranda light, her skin really shone a deep mahogany, gold. It looked smooth and welcoming. I lit my own cigarette and we toasted our new drinks. It was carefree. Baxter was frank and forward, and Maria was responding well. They asked us to escort them across town to the other side of the bay, and join them for further drinks. I relented, to Baxter's delight, and we went along the sparsely lit path. I had a biting buzz, by then, and my face felt warm and my muscles felt loose. The girls skipped and danced in front of us, like sirens reeling us in to danger. It was pleasant. Baxter elbowed me in my side, so I'd look at him, and he smiled wide until I could see his back molars. He definitely thought this was a sure-fire score, and I was glad he was having such a fun time his first night in town. The girls played coy, and hid in dark shadows before jumping out and crashing into us; there were some good laughs. We continued our descent into the darker, quieter part of town and came upon Maria's coastal abode. It was a quaint, adobe-styled house, well-maintained, and had a European villa-esque look. She put on a few lights to reveal a lowered seating area, opened the
French doors, and led us to an outdoor patio that overlooked the sea. She instructed us to wait here and have some smokes. To our delight, she launched a firepit built into the center table
and played some smooth Jazz music.

The music really had me set in a positive mood. Baxter looked at me and nodded in approval. "Impressive," he said. American girls had gradually lost their luster over the past ten years, and their electronic music really turned me off. Maria and Layla had a fresh quality that struck a place deep in our characters. Here and now, I began to understand why Baxter had been so engrossed in the scenery at first arrival. The limits had not been set for this place, just quite yet. American consumerism had not wrought its chains across the lands and seas of the California Sur. And for this, we were glad.

Maria and Layla glided to the patio and took seats beside us, respectively. They had made serious mixed drinks, with tequila and Kahlúa coffee liqueur. We discussed high and low culture, and found joy in related experience. Maria had been steadily acting on the mainland and had a new pilot set to air on a Mexican network at the end of the month. She had a petite frame for such long legs but still could resemble a scaled-down Coke bottle. She asked if she should get implants, that they could further her career.

Baxter fiercely opposed the idea, and Layla and I shared laughter over his reaction. Maria fell melodramatic, put her hand on her forehead and posed as if she was to faint, Ay Dios Mio. We continued laughing, and Maria jumped into Baxter's arms. Layla led me to get more drinks inside where we struck lips and felt all over each other against the bar counter. She tasted supple and sweet. She said, "Jerry, would you like to take me home?" And I replied, "I thought you'd like to take me home."

She turned away, so I could look at her wholesome behind, and lifted a leg as she turned to look at me. Lust really had a way with that image. She fixed me another Brave Bull, and began to gather her coat and purse. She turned off her mobile, and that's where she had me caught. Just as I finished my drink, I urinated and washed

my hands and face in the bathroom. She hid
by the front door, in the wavering lights, and must've enjoyed my
drunken emergence from the bathroom. I looked down the hall to
take a glance outside and saw Baxter clearly occupied by Maria. I
heard the ignition of a lighter and saw Layla's figure leaned back
against the doorframe, like a harlot out of any crime noir. She wig-
gled some keys in her other arm, and waited for me to embrace
her.

Out on the street, Layla skipped to the middle of the road, still
wiggling her keys. She smiled at me and waved the keys towards a
vintage Chevy parked nearby. I followed her every
move, her heels clicking to the pavement. This was a treat—driving was the thing I missed most from stateside. She told me to
go up the coast and on the first road, veer inland. This would take
twenty minutes and once I veered inland, to wake her. The Chevy
bounced rhythmically as the road became bumpier and darker.
The moon rippled across the calm sea to guide our route along
with the headlights. I played music within my head to maintain focus and chain-smoked to keep alert. The car leaned naturally along
the bends, the way older cars feel closer to the driver than the new
computer ones of recent years.

Upon waking her, Layla guided me on a route deep into the
hills and we rose higher and higher from the coast. Forest overtook the road, branches leaning across above and crickets hum-
ming in the night. The roads were dirt and the Chevy tires
gathered and threw stones in our wake. The winds seemed
stronger here, as if they came from a different source than the
coast. I began to notice the road was getting wetter, and here,
we had reached the ranch. The forest cleared to a great pasture,
fenced by decaying wood, and a great stone gate. I couldn't make
out the name of the ranch, but we went along and rose to the hills.

No house was visible from the gateway, yet I obeyed the road and made way. She clicked a button when it was still dark wayward, and then I saw the garage door open. She told me to park the car outside of the garage and through the garage we'd make our way into shelter. Based on the shadows, the house had to be two or three stories, one suited for a Don, a commandeer of great lands.

Layla remained silent other than encouraging me to have no fear. I remained resilient, yet have to admit this mystery was clearly growing the farther we ventured from town. Through the garage, we were again outdoors and gathered dust as we made our way to the back door. She guided me up some stairs and told me to make myself comfortable, as she went to gather wine from the cellar. I considered that I had stumbled upon a true Spaniard descendant. This land alone was indicative of wealth. Up the stairs were a balcony and some French doors leading to darkness. I chose to stand and smoke rather than sit and wait. She brought glasses and a Hungarian red wine, aged twenty years. It was rather tart, just the right amount, and she buried her hair against my chest.

She was awfully romantic but I certainly liked it. Hadn't had a proper woman's touch in some time. We left the glasses on the deck, and she brought the bottle and me into the dark house. The floors were stone, probably marble by the sound, and then I lost her. She lit a candle down the hallway and there we made love in a great bedroom. It was grand. I still was rather disoriented with where I was and once the candle went out, I was completely in the dark.

Sex could be the most sobering of activities. By the time we were ready to call it a night, the day had started but I lacked the care to worry about how I'd return to town. Sleep was soothing.

About midday I awoke to the sun above and the sound of water running. I could hear a fountain or a spring outside, and it was peaceful. Layla was nowhere to be found immediately, and I found a note in proper cursive English by the nightstand. She had gone out and would be back with a warm meal for me. What a nice girl. The time on the note read just past an hour ago, so I washed my face and had a cigarette as I explored the great house. There were no pictures in the hallway, but I did see some great wooden chests through an open door. Seemed no one was home, and I wondered about Layla's abuela.

The thought was fleeting, and I finished the rest of the wine we had left out. Down the hallway, I retraced my steps from the night past and before the stairs, I could look down at the grand living room. The furniture was old but regal and the coffee table looked heavy like the floor of a wooden ship. I spotted a bookshelf and ignored the books, instead, focused on the shelves of the black and white photos. The fact the photos were black and white made the place seem older, and there I viewed a beautiful Hispanic family, with lots of brothers and sisters, and spotted a young Layla on the right side. She must have been a teenager when it was taken. The next photo was of a sturdy man with a great moustache, who kind of resembled Stalin if only he was a Spaniard. He stood strong next to the Chevy I had driven the night before and the license plate said Diego. This had to be the Don, su padre. My assumptions she was of class were right on the mark.

Making my way into the kitchen, I noticed the pots and pans above the center island were new and spotless, and that the plates and silverware were luxurious. The refrigerator was well stocked with beer and I treated myself to a cool Belgian import. I basked in the great ranch view from the kitchen bay window. The green fields extended in all directions. The forest trees bordered the road and wrapped around behind the fields. And up above the treetops, the sloping mountains protected the ranch haven. A strong stream ran through the trees and across the fields. Irrigated canals punched some water to the ranch, and made up a creek. I noticed a well in the distance near the background trees.

I heard the rumble of the Chevy approaching the ranch and was glad when I saw her rush to greet me. We dined, and I did not ask any personal questions and she did not reveal any information to me. She looked even better in the daylight, and for a little while, I felt relaxed. She sensed my restlessness and desire to return to town, and threw me some keys. There was an old Range Rover in the shed I could use, as long as I took down her number and promised to see her when she got back into town. I remained confused about whether or not her abuela was on the premises, but I let my curiosity remain silent. She handed me instructions on how to get back to town, and they were simple enough to follow. Before I left, we kissed passionately and she smelt great.

The Range Rover handled well but the engine growled like it had been lifeless for too long. The way back was quite a sight in the sun, and I even saw a car or two pass in the opposite direction. I did not think much of the night past, for I did not want to consider too much and screw up the fine situation I found myself in. She had given me the exact right balance of push and pull, making me feel wanted but not making me feel needed. The car was a sure prize. I drove onto the main road and veered to a slow stop at Jose's. Rollins was at the bar counter, I was pretty sure, based on the dark black hair and sturdy frame slouched onto an elbow. Had to have been a disaster at the tables last night. Rather than stop in, I found a safe place to park the car, so I could see it outside the hotel window. Luckily, Baxter was nowhere on the route to my room, and here I could wash up in peace. I found a note I must have passed over stuck to my shoe from Baxter—Your phone must be dead. Let's meet at the bar before nightfall.

By the time I made my way to the bar, Rollins was plastered and found me on the veranda after he soiled himself in the bathroom. "Jerry, you douche, where were you last night? I was left stranded at the tables. Lost over five hundred." I waited before I responded so he could self-regulate his behavior. Rollins stumbled into the seat across the table and composed himself, barely.

"Baxter found these girls and I ended up not too drunk at the end of it all."

"Oh, why, then you have an excuse. I guess the sex must have been worthwhile."

"You up for another game with luck tonight? I could use a healthy gamble."

"No, fuck no, I can't afford it. I'm getting destructive again." At least Rollins was self-aware. Sure, he kept me in check when I'd start losing my cool, but as far me taking his reins, there were always serious consequences. Rollins was a cage fighter. He used to compete for money, and but truly, it was for sport, back in the States. The army drilled him and broke him down into a robot. He did not feel physical pain past the age of twenty. Now, I could see, I had to get more plastered and belligerent than he tonight so he'd maintain some semblance of a civilized nature. I anticipated Baxter's arrival and thought, I'd have two hot-heads in my associated company. The locals could tolerate Rollins, he was known around the area, but Baxter was an outside in these parts. Tonight, obligatory supervision was required for them.

"You know, Rollins, maybe you should take a break off the booze tonight. Help luck come back to you. How 'bout it?"

"No, man, you see, I've already hit the high watermark. My drunk will carry me into the night, and with a brief nap when the sun goes down, I'll be perfect for a healthy stream as we take hold of the tables."

"Mickey, you're gonna black out. Your eyes are already blood-shot, and I feel like the air here is ten degrees warmer just by being in an arm's length from you."

"Cut it out, seriously, don't test me. I'm not here to get lectured by a civilian." When he started with the names that separated he from non-soldiers, I knew it was enough. Calling him by his first name must have bothered him. It made him feel the way it felt when his father used to berate him. I lit a cigarette and proposed we take some shots before he head off to rest. We struck glasses and balance was restored. I stared at Rollins, and I had to look away, as his complexion screamed bloodlust. Down the road, I focused on a group of young hombres playing football in the street and saw the makings of a fight develop over an argument after a goal. Closer to the bar, there was no quick action. I peaked over my shoulder and spotted Baxter with Maria across the street. That hellhound looked too happy.

"Briggs, is that your friend over there, Berk-, no I mean, Back-ster with that skinny little thing? Across the street, you see, he's all over that broad."

"Yeah, it appears so. And they appear to be headed to the hotel."

"What a guy, on a marathon from the night before."

"He's one of those quick-to-elope types. Always loved a right-eous adventure."

"He should join us at the tables tonight. My man, Benito, will be real happy to see me tonight. You would've been proud. I didn't even threaten anyone last night, despite my misfortune. I saw a few cartel-types and thought it best I swallow my pride."

"That's complete bullshit. If you saw a few and didn't threaten anyone, they must've been your chaps, in some sense."

"Yep, yeah, okay, you got me. I have a mutual relation of respect with those guys. You already know why."

"Didn't you help them in some form of street justice? Or no, you paid them off."

"How dare you accuse me of bribery? What kind of man of honor would do such a thing? No, the first guess was right. They needed help due to their drunkenness and I was happy to help. Didn't even know they were cartel guys. The stupid nobody tried to steal some of my cash, too, so we were already on the same side. I have principles, a moral code, Jerry. Anyway, like I was saying, Benito will be happy to see me, I'm always one of his most encouraging and reliable customers."

"Reliable is stretching it, man. Be easy on yourself."

"Screw you and your seeming sober semblance. Tonight, I'm not holding back against you. You want me to front you some insurance cash just in case you lose all yours too fast?"

"Enough with your wallet, let's take another round of shots, so you can get out of my face."

"Cabrón, you damn cabrón. Ah, that tequila is spicy. Anyway, here's my spare key. Come wake me, cause I don't trust myself." I would've been opposed but I had the car so his apartment wasn't too far. I consented, and I chuckled as I saw Rollins stagger down the street, waving and shaking hands like he was an important local figure. Man, that fellow really was living his dream. With Baxter busy, I walked towards the docks to go to my favorite taco stand and refueled. I realized I had left my mobile at the hotel and hastily returned. The streets seemed more active than usual, and I remembered, I still had that assignment for the event this weekend. I just returned to my room, when Baxter started knocking aggressively. "Jerry! Jerry!" I lit a smoke before I opened the door, and Baxter fell onto my bed. "Ohhh, Jerry. I think I'm in love. What do I do? What do I do? I got the wedding to go to, and oh I just can't have this end. Not so suddenly."

"So you're in love, again, dear Baxter."

"Don't patronize me. This time, I tell you, it's different. It's real. I feel alive when I'm with Maria."

"You've known her for almost a full day. Get a hold of yourself. Anyway, take a break from her tonight. We're going gambling." Baxter rubbed his eyes excessively and rose from the bed. He stretched his arms and they touched the ceiling. I noticed, he still had the same clothes on as the night before.

"A break's a good idea. A break's a real good idea. You know, I know just what I will do. I'll go gambling with ya'll and then go over to her place after, make some winnings love."

"Don't break your back, boy. She didn't seem like the loose type. Give her some space."

"It's not that. I'm just so enamored. This one, she's righteous, Jerry, I tell you."

I paused. "Hey, Bax, listen, meet me at the bar in an hour, and show up. You were nowhere to be found before sundown."

"Hey, she's still in my room. You can count on me, Jerr. See you then."

My mobile had multiple missed calls and text messages from Bax. One from Rollins, too, and a scenic picture from an unknown number I assumed to be Layla's. She was in Los Angeles. Her mystery grew the more she crossed my mind. I went over my notes for my first assignment and quickly wrote out a first draft for the article. The zine wanted me to showcase Baja California as a place for Americans to travel to, to downplay the danger of the lawlessness of Mexico and to highlight the fact the peninsula was separate from the mainland. Was hogwash, but the zine paid well. So I gave them what they wanted. By the time I had finished, it was just past an hour and I went to meet Baxter at Jose's.

Baxter wasn't there, and I met Maria who was there on his behalf. She informed me he was on an international call to his relatives. I knew the information would be passed on to me soon and so I enjoyed Maria's company. She was rather quiet but made it clear she was interested in me. I reiterated Brent's interest in her and she deflected these remarks with ease.

"Can you tell me anything more about Layla, señorita?"

"Ah, Señor Briggs, you have a thing for that one?"

"Something, clearly. She lent me a car."

"Haha, she does that when she likes to see a man more than once." Her attitude shifted subtly to a more malicious nature. Women and their competition. I discounted her remarks but still was entertained. "You see, Jerry, she's of the high class, like me, but has so much going on in so many different places. Where is she now? Los Angeles, is it?" She stroked my hair, and adjusted her seat closer to mine.

"As you know, last night was the first encounter and I think we all had fun, no?"

"I'll be your guardian for the time being. Brent's such a doll, but he's very forthcoming. I bet it scares off American girls."

"You'd be surprised. They covet that faith more than most."

"Anyway, I'll leave a note at the bar counter for him, and you can drive me home."

"Wait, wait. I have to do something first, pick up a friend."

"They can wait." And off she went inside. Beautiful women and their insidious drive. It's impossible to stop. I jotted down another note and told Brent to wait for me at the bar, that I'd be back with Rollins soon, as to prevent a likely barrage of messages to my mobile. I stood up and approached the counter. Maria latched arms with me and I took her to the car.

She had more zeal than Layla, I could tell already. Some wild animal nature in that petite frame. Her breasts looked larger than I had remembered. On the radio, she turned to a rap station and put the volume down so we could only hear low bass and piercing hi-hats. I noticed her jewels shimmering in the moon and street-lights and they were ornate like those of New York girls. She was quite glad I remembered where she lived, and my thoughts were spot on. Rollins' apartment was closer and he could be picked up on my way back to Jose's. Maria did not wait for me to display any chivalry, and I liked that. She leaned over and climbed on top of me in the driver's seat, and we kissed. I knew I was in the wrong to Baxter but I quickly threw this concern out of my conscience. Her deceptive curves were revealing themselves to me and it turned me on. Just like that, she put me in her grasp and she raised the volume on the music. Her thrusts coincided with the beat and it only lasted a few minutes. She really had caught me off guard. She told me come on now and have a drink with her inside. I wasn't as shocked at her behavior as I was at the strange, somewhat episodic nature of the past few days since Baxter's arrival. How long could this atmosphere persist or perhaps grow and evolve into some type of permanence?

Coming out of her room in a silk robe, Maria went to the kitchen and I could hear her voice as on an intercom. It was sexy. "It's not out of the ordinary for Layla and I to share men. Don't take this the wrong way, Jerry, you clearly can show me more as can I to you, but I want to tell you this for your sake. Sharing men enhances our freedom and such that we are free to choose which is preferred by the other."

"What if you both choose the same?"

"Then it's up to the man, as it should."

She came by with the same cocktails as the night before, and I happily received.

"So I'm a test subject under review, right now? Is that it, señorita?"

"Haha, Jerry, you have more balls than Brent. Relax. Just look at it this way, Layla would be happy for you to be keeping her best friend company while she is all alone in Santa Rosalía. It's a sign of good faith."

Rather than reply, I sipped my drink and lit a cigarette.

"Tell me about your upcoming pilot."

"Ah, I'm so glad you asked, it's a soap opera, and I'm the mystery girl. I won't tell you the title, because I'm not really fond of it, but anyway, there is a secret government agency, the lead plays a spy questioning his loyalties, and I'm the girl that incites his changes in thought and behavior."

"Are you evil?"

"Well, the pilot is only the first episode, we have to wait for it to get picked up. But if I could envision the growth of my character, I'd like to be good, and then turn evil for a while, before revealing some sort of justice in the end, so I think I'm good overall."

"Naturally, of course, a heroine in a violent man's world."

"Something of that sort. Now, Jerry, I'd like it if you kept me company these next few days."

"And as for Brent?"

"The more and more he sees me, he'll get scared I'll grow disinterested and so he'll skip town early rather than late. Don't underestimate the cunning of an actress."

"If you say so."

"Now, make love to me once more, and get on your way. You don't want to keep your friends waiting."

It took me longer than I expected to finish and my lateness kept adding up. Rollins was not too hard to wake and we met Baxter at Jose's. When he asked what had took so long, I said I had trouble finding the gas station, which I did. He kept going on and on about his infatuation with Maria, and Rollins and I told him to quit it. That hopeless romantic nonsense really did not sit well with us. Anyhow, we parked the car and made our way to Benito's. Benito greeted Rollins with a hearty warmth and sat us at one of the more well kept tables. Now, I really understood why Rollins always said the locals could pick up on a newcomer's discomfort. The mining facility windows and doors were all shut, the ventilation system had to be jammed from dirty filters, and the sweat boiled up in such a stuffed hole. It was as if we were in the middle of an engine, all oil devoid, and the impending heat hinted at explosion at any possible

future. I wasn't getting any luck off the draw and thereby played a game of patience until fortune started favoring me. Baxter was aggressive off the bat. On the second or third hand, he was definitely bluffing, according to me, but the other players were unfamiliar with his style and let him have an early take at some winnings. He did a poor job of masking his surprise and bought the table two rounds of drinks in celebration. His overt positivity was surely a sign of vulnerability and the locals lured him in as easy prey. Rollins played a conservative style, not as patient as I but closer to mine than to Baxter's. Benito came by every ten minutes or so to check up on his favorite foreign customer and eventually Rollins took a break to go into a back room with Benito.

The night was less hectic so far than I had expected. I was grateful to Benito, for he was monitoring Rollins by chance and I was only left with Baxter to look out for. Baxter's stack of chips kept piling up and his luck had to spoil soon. Luck remained elusive to me, and so I journeyed to the back room where Rollins had went with Benito. There, I discovered a makeshift bar and smoking room, with a garage door open that led to the docks. The square outline of the garage led to a far horizon point on the sea and it was striking to the eye. Here, I did not see Benito or Rollins and assumed they had gone up the stairs by the bar counter to a private office. Rollins quickly spotted me from above and hastened me up the stairs.

Benito was a Cartel associate, by trade, and an intimidating Mexicali, by nature. He wasn't necessarily large or even mean in the face. It was his hands, looking like broken leather, and snarly voice that gave me a cautious approach. Not to mention the machetes and guns that were in clear visibility behind his desk. Leaned back in his armchair, Benito strummed an acoustic guitar with masterful skill and smoked a cigar. He asked if I'd be staying in town for a while and when I told him it'd be at least another week, he encouraged me to come by the tables more often. "Rollins tells me you're a compadre from birth. I could tell immediately and I am glad. Your other fellow, down there, clearly a different breed and birthright. He needs to be careful." I thanked him for his candid remark and we all shared an ancient tequila I still never have come across again.

Rollins' judgment that his daytime drunk would put a ceiling on his drunkenness for the night seemed to be holding true. I tell you, if any man could be called a tank, it was Rollins. An indestructible force of nature, incessant blood flow and heart palpitations. Skin like a rhino. And a willpower like a wrecking ball, a juggernaut more akin to a caveman brute strength than any civilized training. It still amazed me to this night. Benito and Rollins began to escalate their voices to a kiddy, comedic nature all on the subject of the effects of methamphetamine. This troubled me after I saw Rollins smoking a pipe with it. No wonder his temperament was not on the blackout drunk side. Mixing depressants and stimulants always had a way of betraying a man's nature and I had avoided doing so since my college days. Anyway, Rollins could take care of himself, as long as he did not lose his cool. Benito asked if Rollins and I would care for some sample hallucinogens, peyote, and we took them with gratitude. On one condition, that the peyote was for us and us alone, not the other Americano. Consider this a gift and sign of respect. We accepted his offer. Rollins noticed my lack of energy, or rather his influx of energy, and got Benito to spark a joint and settle the air. I took a few hits and could taste the harshness of the strain. It burnt my mouth but I showed no sign of discomfort. The cannabis set me back on intensity and I began to notice my heart wavering from fast to slow, slow to fast. I thanked Benito for his hospitality and made my way back to the tables.

Baxter had lost most of his winnings. The glaze on his eyes had carried over to his face and I noticed sweat dripping from his scalp to his neck. His back was soaked when I patted him on the shoulder for support. Fortune had started to miss me and the tables began feeding me luck for my patience. By now, smoke had blanketed the room, and the cloud had descended to the green felt. The other tables were filled now to the brim, spectators encroaching on every player's move. Melodic whims of despair and glory echoed and collided with the dormant machinery surrounding. My vision started to multiply and my pupils must have been dilated. Fists pounded the table as the blinds grew larger and the stakes more costly. The stacks of chips bounced with the fists and shifted like Jenga pieces from an earthquake. Rollins returned, wound up, spun and aggressive. Out of the corner of my eye, I mistook him for Baxter, and this change of pace carried through the other players.

Rollins won a hand on the river and his fists collapsed everyone's stacks of chips, like dominoes in wake of an avalanche. I exclaimed for him to cool it and he glared at me with malice. Don't curb my high, don't you dare bring me down, he looked. Baxter's shit-eating grin resurfaced on the next hand. He bought more drinks for the players and his winnings began to return. At this point, it was approaching the twilight hours and I thought it best to cash out. At the cashier's desk, Benito informed me my timing was spot on, and that it would be best to get the two loco Americanos out of the place before chaos could take hold. I agreed, and at Benito's glare, Rollins cashed out, but Baxter remained ignorant at the tables. We let him play one more hand, which he won, and upon looking for his friends, could not find them, left the tables and found us at the desk with Benito. Benito was quite cordial and professional and paid Baxter his winnings accordingly.

We exited the premises with Rollins covering our backs. I drove Rollins home and Baxter asked me to take him to Maria's. I got lucky that I did not have to convince him it was a bad move, he figured it out for himself, and instead, we went back to the hotel. The next day, I did not see Baxter. He was not in his room, or at Jose's, or anywhere else nearby. Rollins told me we should save the peyote for the weekend and I agreed. I conducted some research on my laptop about the upcoming event I had to cover, and realized it had been cancelled. My boss still had not informed me, and with my winnings at the tables, I had enough to cover my expenses for the next week without taking any funds from the magazine. I was in the clear. As the hours passed, I realized this was the first day I was not drinking continuously. It didn't feel good or bad. It was just an observation. I changed this behavior to prevent it from turning into a trend or a pattern and planted myself in bed with a bottle of American whiskey for variety's sake.

I heard some boats motoring into port from my window and considered the state of affairs from the past few days. The duo of Maria and Layla confused me. I was locked in to seeing Layla again as I had her car. I dreaded the thought of returning to the house and finding not her but her abuela there and having to hold myself accountable. Who were these women and how was I so draw in to their web of seeming lies and deception? In any case, these feelings of dread were fleeting and I jockeyed myself back into a normal masculine stance. They were beyond good-looking, easy going, and were well taken care of. There were no threats of past men in sight and I seemed to have a tryst with one and an arrangement with the other. Anyway, I was leaving next week, if not earlier, so I could always consider this an enjoyable memory of a foreign love when I was back in America. Still, though, I could not help but think there was a lot more than my surface assessment to be uncovered.

The whiskey put me to sleep early, and the clouds overcast the sun in the morning. It was Friday, and I thought of going to see Maria. Baxter had left a note with the concierge, informing me of his departure and that he'd be back next week after the wedding. Womanly company could be swell, but I remembered Rollins had that peyote. I had the car so we could go trip at Layla's. I decided the abuela had been a safe explanation for Layla to recount and that the abuela was absent from the premises. It was a safe bet and the ranch was isolated from people but close enough in case we wanted to reintegrate into the town during the comedown. I purposefully instilled positive thoughts as the clouds cleared, ate a hearty breakfast and telephoned Rollins that today we should sample Benito's treats. He agreed and said to pick him up at half past noon. I refrained from drinking in the morning, instead stocking up on supplies for the trip to come.

Not new to hallucinogens, I acquired biological components that could ensure our trip would be a success. A carton of Marlboros, a case of beer, four liters of spring water, and four pounds of ground meat. Also, a block of cheese, two loaves of bread, and an assortment of spices. Coupled with my notebook computer for music, the day was set for success. I admit I was excited to feel some seminal connection to the cosmos that only a hallucinogen can activate, and the timing was rather perfect. Rollins was waiting for me on the street and off we went up the coast and inland through the trees.

The ranch was just as majestic as it had been and was vacant. Here, the mountain air was cooler and the sun was soft with the scattered clouds. Rollins remarked I sure had stumbled onto an aristocratic one with the car and ranch, and that it could not have worked out any better for the both of us now. We unloaded the truck and set the supplies in their according places, on the outdoor table, the dining room table, and the food and drink in proper storage. The grill was gas-powered and looked brand new. I checked to make sure it worked and then plugged in my computer to an outdoor socket. Rollins told me that peyote was from a cactus, and that the slices provided by Benito could be more potent than any magic mushroom we encountered stateside. He said they were used for rituals by locals and that the effects have a strong impact with human contact in a natural environment. He warned me not to underestimate their potency.

We ate the slices and they were god-awful bitter. Rollins pulled out a large bag of cannabis that he had picked up from Benito the other night we were gambling. On the come up, we smoked two joints and listened to low frequency recordings with jazz samples and tribal drums. The mood carried to the fields and the grasses synced in harmony with the drums and the wind. We were silent and let the peyote take hold. I could feel my organs more and more, the blood coursing through my veins. I took off my socks and planted my bare feet on the wooden deck. Staring at my feet, they seemed to merge with the wood and the creases in the wood looked the same, vascular and pulsing. We began chainsmoking and other than the movements of our arms and mouths, we were statuesque.

The rhythm of the music increased, and in unison, Rollins and I readjusted our positions. Every move seemed to have more gravity and the wood felt softer and softer against the soles of my feet. A lightheaded ease overcame my sense of balance and my bones felt absent, disintegrated. The cigarette smoke lingered in front of my eyes in a soothing wave across the country landscape. A few birds flew overhead towards the road from which we came. The fields seemed to shrink as my conscious state was overrun by an inward focus. The kick of hallucinogens was that you always could not escape your perspective. Any recursive stimulus was hypersensitive to the body and the interplay between action and reaction meshed into a singular experience. The back of my throat was numb and my jaw seemed to elongate. Breathing was secondary to mental inclinations and the idea of clarity was at the forefront of feeling within an hour.

Rollins traveled into the field in front, leaving the music and me behind. It was a pleasurable sight. I had my own cinematic scene to view and noticed he pulled out a pistol from his backside. It had to have less than twelve rounds, so I turned off the music and made sure to count each shot he took. He could be trusted. He wasn't drunk. I ignited the grill and began preparing the beef with spices. The slippery meat left a membranous coat on my fingertips and the spices stuck concurrently. I wielded a knife to cut the vegetables and it looked glorious with refracted waves of light against the blade. I threw the meat on the skillet and they crackled in the heat. Out beyond, Rollins tried to shoot at birds, I thought, and was unsuccessful. He then swayed in the breeze and set up a large barrel as a target. From my vantage point, I saw he had shot a few holes in the barrel, and now the liquid inside was seeping out. This must have been a great sight, as he stopped his shooting and was inspecting the flow of the damage.

I left the grill running and quickly sprung out to where Rollins was. The barrel had sand and the flow was pleasant, constant, like an hourglass. We were both on our hands and knees inspecting the cataracts of sand, and I let one sand stream fall onto my hand and fall to the ground through the ridges of my fingers. We remained silent and I returned to the grill just in time to prevent the meats from burning unevenly. I wasn't particularly hungry, but the act of cooking was a sight in itself. Rollins had disappeared the next time I looked at the barrel. I heard the music again and assumed he was in close proximity. The wooden deck leaned downward as if pulled by the gravity of human force.

Rollins appeared again on the fields and looked feral. Not that he was running to and fro but that his hair was unkempt, his arm-sleeves pulled up to his pits, and his skin resembled fur from a distance. A two-legged horse. I looked at my hands and they beamed with life. The meats oozed when I knifed them and had a healthy pink complexion, medium rare. After the cheese coated right, we ate and the act of chewing was momentous. The peak was yet to come but I could not imagine a more pleasurable feeling. The sun had shifted west and I checked the clock on the computer. It had only been three hours.

I proposed a journey by car and Rollins thought it a swell idea. After the meal, we approached the truck. It looked too small for us to fit in but as we got nearer the size adjusted appropriately. The engine grunted upon ignition and from the windows, the sights were framed in rectangular order. We ventured into the world and the trees looked inverted, from greens at the treetops and branches extending to the ground in a cobweb like fashion. At the coastal road, we saw workers walking back to the town and they looked like ants, remote from interaction and the force field of the car's wake. We felt merry and carefree, impervious to any threats or concerns.

We stopped at Rollins' apartment to end the driving episode. We didn't feel like going out with the commoners and remained inside. Rollins was a luxurious man, of privilege, and the apartment looked too well kept to be in a small Mexican village. It felt safe to be in such a living space. He told me he wanted to shower and that he'd be a while so I should find something to do. I refused to turn on the television, for fear of being hypnotized, and instead, I stared at the roofs of the neighboring buildings. Rollins' dog interrupted my focus and I pet the beast for some time, appreciating the velvet-like fur.

An eerie buildup of vertigo started to overtake me, and to combat and eliminate this threat, I slowly wielded my muscles and stared down at my hands, squeezing them into and out of fists. I leaned my head back and stared at the wooden ceiling and smoked a cigarette, letting the smoke reside in my lungs for an extended period for each puff. The disoriented feeling kept building. This habitat was a buffer zone from the outside world; it was not aligned or as they say, meant to be, in such a place. Rollins' absence only helped this feeling persist, and to escape this realization, I shut all the windows, and closed the doors to the rooms that had windows. Now, I was in the pitch black hallway, the shower barely audible through the walls and closed doors. Shielding myself from uncontrollable stimuli helped me regain my steadfast ease and comfort. The dark always comforted me since I had come of age, for I felt in control. The space was contained and became dark by my own doing. When I closed my eyes, it was dark, and when I opened them, it was the same. My external limbs, I could feel, but could not see. I imagined I was in a vacuum, neither in space nor in a cave. All I possessed were my thoughts and the weights we call limbs. I considered what it would be like to be blind and how it cannot all be so bad. In such a place absent from light, peace was achieved. It was essentially environment-enforced meditation. The clarity of a black hole.

The running water stopped and this threw me back into reality. A door opened and then another, and a line of natural light outlined the bottom of multiple doors through the hallway. Rollins must have had an intuition that I was in the hallway, as he bypassed entering and went around. I appreciated this and prepared for the daylight. The light pulsated through my body upon contact and the peak of the trip had concluded. My hands looked older and healthier. Rollins was in the window seat, dog by his side, smoking a cigarette. He concurred that the time had passed and we should return to the ranch to gather our belongings. I decided to turn on my mobile and see if I had any messages. Maria was available.

With the truck, I picked her up from her place, and Rollins traveled solo via his motorcycle. He told me he'd find the way back no problem. I wasn't worried. Maria was less energized than the night times I had seen her. She knew I was on something and perhaps I acted different in that capacity. The fading natural light made her appear more gold than the night and when her hand stroked the back of my ear, it tickled. On the dirt road off the coast, the tire streak of Rollins' motorcycle guided our path. By the time we arrived, Rollins had prepared some food to our pleasure and I felt spry. After the meal, he declared a need to use the waning effects of the trip for riding. He departed peacefully and as the last sounds of the engine whined in the distance, Maria knotted herself around me.

Coming down from a serious high always took a toll on the body and mind. The way I saw it, the mind could trick the body to ease this comedown. From the peyote to orgasm, my mind was thoroughly occupied and the physical sensation of such a prized woman cancelled out any aches and pains my body felt. From one level of perception to a lower, my appetite was fed. So was hers. Maria didn't talk much and when she did, I managed to bypass what she was saying and focus on another subject. She wasn't bothersome and it was mutual.

I had another week left here. I got drunk, gambled, and played off Maria. There was no real future, here. But I wasn't trying to think, so I went about my business and left on good terms with Maria. When he returned, Baxter was annoying and I cast him off with Rollins. Maria stuck with me. It still feels like a good memory. I left the car with Maria. Layla never came back.

2

A Familiar Accord

The streetcar sat menacing in the failing light. Flickering forms passed by the walkway until the sun fell away and by then, there were no passing forms. The streetlights were late coming on and when they finally came alit, the streetcar looked more menacing. Its black paint blacker than the darkness between the streetlights and shadows. It was parked in such a position that you could not see if passengers were inside. But then the headlights beamed on and you could tell.

Richard Grant emerged from the gaming salon and entered the backseat.

"Here?"

"No," said the passenger. "Santoro's. They're already there. Mel, shall we?"

Mel gave the engine life and then the car motion. The streets were empty save a straggler and a group of youthful miscreants soliciting at a movie theatre. Santoro's appeared closed to the public but the doors gave way when Grant entered, alone.

The passenger said he'd be back to finalize the terms after he attended to another engagement. That's all he said before Mel drove the car away. Santoro's doors closed and Grant did not see a living person.

Shudders of glass and laughter poached the silence and stillness the farther back Grant went. He wanted to make an impression, a fashionable one to establish his experience. He glided slow and controlled and did not knock.

Grant unveiled himself and they knew who he was. He knew they knew who he was but not how he was. To make it sure, he told them what they did not want just the way they could accept it and like it.

"I'll play your fix on three conditions. One, no taxes, cash only. Two, the bartender with the red hair. And three, some tickets to the Yankee game." Smoke was the only sign that the clock kept going. The toilet flushed finally and the one that needed to see it and hear it all had not seen or heard it all, if any.

Buttoning up his pants syncopated with his belt buckle sounding like a metronome, the empty space between the washroom and the gallery area where the seats and the witnesses and Grant were. The mensch that had his feet cocked up and his hands behind his disheveled skull cap had smiled for too long and began to realize it when he faltered and almost considered addressing the post-piss oaf, el jefe.

He caught himself quick, mouth open, mouth close, breathe in, recover and put the hands and feet down slow. This collection did not typify fear. Sensible respect and a penchant for cautious recklessness was more their approach, an individual playing field.

"What makes you think you're the one to demand demands?" the boss asked with unreserved opulence, his head still skewed down ways to inspect the polish of his shoes. No splash marks and no answer. Then, he looked at Grant.

Demands is a strong word, the wrong one to put it plain, and as he said they were mere conditions to himself, he considered if what he had to lose was worth losing face amongst the crew. An impulse shuddered his body and so, he knew it was not worth losing face.

"The only reason you deal with me is because I'm straight reliable and entwined in the neighborhood."

A muffled cough marked the end of his declaration and it came not from the boss or the speaker. The cough gave way to the clang of a glass against wood and the steady stream of wine pouring into glasses to fill again. Matches striking like dynamite ended the pause.

The boss leaned his tugboat body against the wall by the washroom hall and noted the excess smut on the soles of his loafers. He got on his two feet and skidded them deep into the wood so they scraped off the smut, and he primed into a position of attack the way a bull or a horse centers its gravity. The motion towards Grant was slow and purposeful, and he placed his paw around Grant's shoulder like a headlock could be in the works.

Then, they were alone in the front room and raindrops sucked on to the glass on the entrance doors. With the gallop of rain incessant, they could conjure their thoughts into statements and tread careful on each other's egos.

Once the doors from the back room that they had come from had closed, the boss was reaching beyond the counter for clean glasses and Grant was grabbing a bottle from the top shelf because he was tall enough to reach it when motioned to by the boss. Grant glided the bottle across the counter to the boss, who caught it in stride, and glasses were poured and handed.

Before they could toast or drink, the boss clarified, "That racket out the county line has overextended. They think they can encroach and get away with it. Now, we'll let them get away with it, on the surface but under the surface, we'll get 'em."

"What about appearances?"

"What of them?"

"Those guys in there, those guys out there, may not be as patient as you."

"It's not their job. They follow instructions and can moan and groan to their juicy squeezes and sponges."

"Some gallantry being a bootlegger."

"You know that term bothers me."

"You know I know it bothers me."

"Yet you keep on."

"I don't see a long face."

"Just stick around and wait 'til your eyes pulp into melons."

"I'll pass."

"After you shine my shoes."

"Like hell."

The glasses clanged and they drank in unison. The boss took a big gulp and waited for Grant to take it all down.

"Now, no one will die but they will get sick, sick enough to notice and obvious enough for them to notice it was from their brew, but it'll take time."

"I'll cheers to that." The match ember faded as the smoke masked their smiling faces into the cool dim of the lingering shadows. Put out, Grant left into the streetcar waiting, looking menacing to the flooding streets. And the rain had finally stopped.

3

City Country

Forage amongst the weeds and puddling smock of salted copses to get a true atmosphere. For in a land of metal, plastic, and mildew, there requires a certain abstraction to absorb the potency of such surroundings.

A copse in a city is a cluster of buildings. Tenements and cooperative buildings showcase the most nature one can afford without public upheaval. Notice the fluttering pups of meager vigor and the grass so green it might as well be artificial. Carry down the corridor of stoneways wrapping the coppice and you reach the street. The street. The public roads. The sidewalks blocked by legions of wide-hipped stroller pushers, bikers massaging the pavement with tread, smokers shirking their rebellion for all to whale, and when you catch a flurry of young, grit-nub children, you realize this place is merciless to a degree of comedy.

When approaching a main avenue, great causeways for motion, gusting with kitsch vibrato, beware. Never stop when some stranger approaches you with a smile. Never. Exceptions, nie. Stare straight ahead, and if you can change your eyes with shaded spectacles, do so and maintain the disposition of an emperor's bust, as you careen with grounded momentum through the whirlpool of dusty bodies. You will be pleased to experience stragglers and even respectable looking city dwellers, will alter their paths, so as you can maintain yours, like a great yacht hydroplaning the slow fishermen away from the courses of efficiency.

This is one mundane deficiency, rather, characteristic, of a common courtesy I compel to afford you. The cosmopolis is a terrain much foreign to nature in artifice, but upon impulse's coattails, you may find yourself riding a crested wave tidal in torrent and titillation. You may begin to consider yourself a grand player in this masquerade of manic highs and lows, so many shades of man's folly at your gaze that overload is normal.

Enjoy the quiet when you rarely find it, or if you are too hooked, never stop dancing.

4

Knock Yourself Out

Masha spoke smoke. Not that she chained cigarettes. The lisp of her tongue stressed dissonant syllables in words like loquacious and prescient, especially once a few lethal drinks got to circulating her bloodlines. Then, and only then, the flash of rushed life sought to beam through her stained glass eyes, longing to cry out, "I am here, take me if you dare. Tremble at my presence if you must."

Burr and Leek battled for her attention. They both had smooth plays—experience, fortitude, apathy—and they rested on their buttocks like ships at anchor on a waveless bay.

"I wish you were here longer," she declared, and curled a wave of hair behind her left ear, and swung her chin down and around so the hair would stay behind the ear. "Forever," a slight lisp on the last -er, just for effect. The emphasis poached Burr and Leek's hand on her hip, though unseen, was more a move that established the score.

Burr maintained proper smiles and a sigh. It was certain he had carried a deed melancholy drag, for the magic in a body this Masha had bloomed into after years of militant development via dance, only to be released to society as a canvas hinged on bodily beams to be cultivated and caught.

Leek had a multitude of years for a head start. Now, he earned a respectable income, spoke various romantic tongues, and had a glorious beard framing his broad bent features. Many years, he had failed to marry and was just the content social boy friend.

These words do not go together. To be a boy called a friend is one drag. To combine boy and friend is an insult by default. Matrimony is the only respectable form in society.

Burr recognized Leek's folly. Leek's longing expression always showcased an imp's innuendo, "Oh, what am I to do? I am such a grunt, and my luxuries abound, I just want it all." Burr played the monologue in his mind's ear and smirked behind his closed lips.

The glasses were empty and required filling. Masha decided they ought to gamble. "The drinks need decorum." The jagged glasses did seem rather morose in the bright lights of the front of the ballroom where the trio had been, jostling between tomfoolery and arduous respectability.

The event was meaningless, an ordered excuse to be dainty and dignified to the goddesses of vanity in an elaborate myopia of courtship and armour gauging.

Sir Wolfenstein bears a new staff, yet Monsieur Chabon sports a one-of-a-kind surtout custom designed and tailored by the iconoclast Gaultier. Che bello! Yet, have you noticed Lady Lorraine's new companion, what glow in his cheeks, I could guess he has quite the athletic talent. He is one of the cavalry. There are no cowboys on cobblestones, he's an equestrian in competition. The jockeys would eat him alive. Kinesthetics are primitive, please, let's take alternative glances at Señora Ramosanda's bosom. They must be artificial. She clearly wants us to notice that, have you noticed how many instances she chooses to visit the greyhounds for petting. She wants to be pet by the furtive glance. It's quite an art. An art of the matter should express an emotion recessed in the living condition that penetrates heavy and potent, wiping out simplified surface tension. Okay, her technique lacks sophistication, yet you must recognize her plaintive enthusiasm. Let's set up Burr with her. Please, he would never. Who's to say. I am to say, he seeks a like "I." You're excused. What, you enjoy how he looks at me. I do not know such a concept. It makes you feel good about yourself. Due to the cause of my mighty dismay, fickle Miss Calypso of Wonders. Let's go vomit over the terrace, I can't breathe in here.

Burr had smoked four cigarillos consecutive and was fecund at the notice of a long narrow shadow approaching his perch. The way the shadow figured implied a gown adorning an attractive woman. Blessed he considered the moment, as it was Masha. She ran a finger across his shoulders and he passed the fifth cigarillo to her touch hand. He lit a sixth. Silence was cool. Burr thought, where had Leek gone, though he could not dare and ask, it revealed a sign of insecurity and a rush of entangling impropriety if he was to interrogate such a notion.

Masha knew the score and let it ride to the vanishing smoke.

"Wearing a ring on that finger."

This was a stark gesture. She twirled her hand so the glimmer of the jewel reflected via the spotting light from the hall behind and mingled with the spiral of smoke and ember sliding the heirloom with a twinkle.

"A fabled gem—my mother's."

"Now yours."

"It appears so."

"Isn't that bad luck?"

"If I was in advent for a certain ceremony."

"He's never asked?"

"He's never brought it up."

"Is that so?"

"So?"

She glanced with caprice at the man who refused to give a sign suspect of intrigue. See, here was the time for Burr to crack a joke, a bridge of witticism, or farcical banter, to dispel the tension and reset the status quo. He never did that, and she knew, now, how she had come to appreciate his gravitas for her person and presence. They certainly looked splendid side by side. Any assortment of attendees and attendants could assume they were an attachments.

But it was not so and the confines of living comfortable were to see that possibility had never had legs.

"Take me to the floor."

"This number, it's too slow."

"It's just right. It's a long piece, so I'll run along to the powder room for a moment. Please be there." She let the cigarillo burn out on the banister, like all pretty girls. Too gentle to crush a heart.

Emerging where her shadow narrowed into a line before invisibility came a burly force with great shoulders and a blockhead. Guessed right that Leek could not be far behind her motions. He replaced her beside and nudged Burr with a jab charade on Burr's smoke arm. He seized the cigarillo left alit from the banister and exhumed the tobacco as it verged on inactivity.

"Good times."

"You ought to come to the country some time."

"I'd like that; I like the idea of that ..."

"But you cannot envision it actually occurring."

"Not in a timely manner."

"Within reason."

"Seemingly." Leek tapped his fist on the slab and looked at distant staring Burr. "It's quite nice to see you in the city, on the rise, in good health. I'm quite proud to call you, friend, and host you, that you'd call upon me to host you for a majority of your visit."

"We're fine, fellow. Are we not?"

"Have you gotten on the ice?"

"In the white of winter, the river freezes through the trees to a quaint lake overlooking the ranges and one mishmash of a peak. You see, last year, there had been a great fire and the black of the ash stained the peak, so it has a mark of beauty. There must be a flurry of rocks because the snow near hits the mark, and now that it is black and burned, you can see it from afar."

"It must be quiet."

"It's louder in the wilderness than the city."

"When I understand that declaration, I promise to make the journey."

"Bring the dogs."

"Yes."

"Bring your skates."

"Yes."

"Bring your rifle."

"Yes, with certainty."

"Don't bring her." They shared laughs. Burr truly smiled. "She demanded a dance; it's about time."

Leek, not a chance of malice, looked to Burr. Full of mirth for a brother, "knock yourself out." Burr hated him then and loved her spare. What difference did it make? Nothing meant nothing.

5

Natural Purpose

The range was lifeless upon entry. The pallid scent of power and explosion cast an invisible tint on the space. And the way the tube lights struck the shiny shelved instruments should have been perfect in the high lights clouded. It had to be the smoke. Not of the cigarettes still clinging to their purpose but of the nascent aroma lingering in between the glass and the walls.

"How long has it been?"

"Five, not even ten minutes."

"No wonder."

"No wonder, what?"

"Dust in here."

"You and your details. Quit noticing such nonsense."

"There's something about it."

"If you say so."

The duo bypassed the selection chamber and passed to the portal to go in from out. They placed plugs in their ears and broke the membrane to access the gallery.

Even though the dead space where the shots fired to their predisposed fate was dirty with shells and shrouds of targets and related waste, something unnatural was obvious to them both. No concept could mold until now.

Now, Jack Youngston could see it clear for what it was. As he scanned the clearing in front of the cool stream between the slopes covered in naked birch trees bespectacled with melting snow flakes.

The smooth breeze above whistled between the canopies of entangling branches high, lithe in motion easing his looming restless urge from taking too great a grip. He was glad he could see the wind altering the shooting field and he was glad it was not striking him below. He thought he should have worn another layer or two, or maybe some thicker socks because his toes were cooler than he would have preferred.

Ten to fifteen paces to his left, Al Billings lurched back and cracked his spine with a flap of his arms like he held an imaginary accordion. After the crack, he looked as Jack Youngston looked back in understanding.

This waiting was a physical burden. A moment later, disorder sounded as the breaking of near frozen branches and a shuddered tide back to the silence of the cool stream.

"It's a lion," Al whispered. Jack nodded in agreement. That's the only predator that could stalk and ambush with such efficiency stone cold. We were after a different beast altogether, Jack thought to himself, and so, he believed the audible witness to the successful kill was a good omen. The way the birch trees wrapped around the clearing made the clearing seem a crater, gorged with nothing and muddy snow. The stream's tread revealed the tracks fresh and well trodden, and the beast was expected to cross again.

Now, with the lion feeding on the left, a beacon of death, Jack Youngston predicted the beast to showcase a resolve of instinct, and approach from the right. Better to avoid the predator claimed territory. On his shift slightly right, Jack Youngston noticed a cadent shine next to his boot that did not belong there. Upon inspection after little digging and wiping, it came to look obsidian, archaic, elemental. A souvenir to authenticate the specific experience. Another omen, he thought to himself.

But, do two omens cancel each other out, or do they only add on top of each other, to heighten a justified expectation? Or, is the pendulum starting to shift back and a disturbance is up to encounter. Maybe just the thought itself was an omen, good or bad, or both, he could not decide.

He took a long breath to focus on the smoke exiting, only there because he was there exhaling and his body balancing and the surroundings cold. Maybe he could piss and just reset, quit thinking to pass the time. Such trivial pursuits racing in circles going nowhere. His conscience was bothersome, that was an absolute he was quick to admit.

The one thing he did not think about was aiming and firing, as the moose came into range, magnificent legs like masts or pillars standing in defiance of the stream's current. The fall was tragic and harmonious all at once and he knew he did not get the kill shot and that was fine with him and his conscience.

The empty range emerged to the front of his mind and all he could think of was the smell that he barely glimpsed at the ignition of his firearm and how a cigarette would treat him steady. A slow way to kill, to balance out the act committed, a way to give back. Al Billings had one alit and was approaching the carcass, damming the cool stream.

6

To Make Simple

Sara Jane had been a fool. Not by her own analysis but by the way her exiled counter had seen it. She was one akin to feeling the pangs of fortunate love targeted at her soul, governed by a body impregnable to criticism.

Such a man that dare attempt such a petulant debate had already lost any face, save shame, at inception.

So there she had been, bored like those with no vanity as strong as the mirror, so perfect in presentation that content was recognized as a default axiom. Beyond assumptions, beauty is the proof of relevance in a fool's world.

So she was a fool and she had a foolish man who saw to her organic necessities. Food, shelter, fixing furniture, grooming dogs, driving cars, a glorified butler.

Not bad, she thought, her consideration of how far she had come from a dead beach down to the end of the coast to now, receptive to a gaudy loft apartment adorned with luxury focused on emblems of prestige and conditioned dignified airs. She had a court just for being a beautiful fool. She had grown accustomed to it.

So, when the contumely fool of a man believed her to be asking him to construct another court, he was pouncing at full throttle. Then, she turned heads and declared love for the laborer.

This greatly troubled naïve man. He followed his heart, for he had never come so close to uniting soulless ecstasy. Just by thinking it, by saying no, she had considered the possibility. If it were different, if the timing was more right, if it felt like the right time. Impregnably admitting to her desire.

Excusable was her gaze. Tragically, he hadn't the time to wait. He was prime for a co-pilot. Take it or no, she already left it. So, to make things tidy, he declared his love, and that she was a treacherous spinster. He had thought her sagacious but she was, in truth, a bottomless slug that used beauty to comport accepting smiles. A blossoming flame that froze upon touch. By and large, she was safe from pain because he acted as the reject. He wished her well, and the moral of such a story comes like this.

After two weeks, if you don't care, you used her.

7

Standard Exception

A lex expected nothing. Not so in the way of cynics nor in the mindset of swashbucklers. For, the world had been erected on an immovable platter, and henceforth, spoils were limited and the means to collect such spoils proved arbitrary and facetious.

The world Alex knew was a world of occasional social upheaval, unrest, policy change, and surface peace, so to settle. War was a Jonathan Edwardian axiom never exercised. Still so, the specter of 'what if,' loomed over the individual the way a plague reeks its detriment to the resultant innocents. The day presented light, and promise permeated pleasant airs. "Cool takes to those who have the proper attitude." An exchange with the visitor, Martin.

"What cool does today hold?"

"A cold warmer than feline bosom and blankets of fur."

"Fat chances."

"Indeed, they are more likely than not."

"I see nothing in the interim."

"Orient yourself to the long view."

"So to speak?"

"So to say."

"Come again."

"The long view."

Distance, relative perspective, possible comprehension. Conjecture's mighty deck. In all, assumption usurps fact. For in what ways, intonations, hesitations, sarcasms, does the beating heart attempt brazen connection shameless and lost. No holds bar, the judges, or critics, circumvent the effect, and objectify its greater picture, beyond mere commoners' explications.

Alex had prior commitments. Hence, he required sleep. Such as the encumberment of the blood pumped cadaver, strained by agents of myriad forms, and permutations entwined with ill definitions. Martin, fatigued, approaching the limit that patient disillusionment admits to folly, carried his headstrong content into dreams surface sunken and conscience embedded. Harm expired and hope reigned into a sprouting specter of canonical fission.

For, taking considerations vast in time space and brief in summation, Alex and Martin shared true care and better yet, complemented one another's misgivings. Henceforth, ambitions alit into a great conflagrate flame knew no gravitational bound. They were to rise, and due to a sullied wisdom, wings of eagles united, disciplined, and slipshod, were fireproof. Fuel was abstraction sundried to an organic tranquility.

The duo had a collaboration under way. Sharded by logistics, cocooned for a suspended orbit, creativity loomed as Lady Fortuna, going, goes, gone, on the homestretch of an infinite generational race.

"We tend to have good timing."

"Aye."

8

A Stormy Backdrop

The forded waters cracked and clawed at the bowl of the valley, like jovial turks clutching for winning tickets at county fairs and at city exchanges. The wind bursts guised the ambience with stifles of suspense, cycloning around the reverberations of the waves. Never did the wind spur the water to fill the bowl. Only the rain could do that. And the trees with leaves dropping minute drips like those for eyes.

It was on such a windy day that the trees seared of beechwood and birch identities caught waters composed by the black sky graded to cool charcoals and lugubrious purples as the sun strutted evasively to mix the palette. The gaunt tree that once was a towering watcher was now leaning passed strength and the imminent fall was bound to happen on such a day of storm.

The human error can speed up chaos. So it was for a young lad by name of Van who had been chosen into a situation of consequence. His three compatriots, all aged younger than beards or beers, urged him onto the tight rope of the leaning watcher.

"Farther, farther."

"That's it."

"Keep going."

"You have it."

"Don't worry."

"This is spectacular." Once this was said by the quietest specta-tor, the mise-en-scène cast heightened contrast, the sun vanished, the blacks more stark, the brightness substituted with negative space. Van's heart palpitated, the pallor of his face white on sweat on wood and leaves, and the tree shook. The forded waters below taunted with crass evidence, always the same in spite of the condi-tions. His shadow had appeared obnoxious, he thought, prodding out unnatural to the tree the farther and farther he traversed.

Then the bellows of shrieking thunder and the symphony had begun. The shaking, the swaying, the roots standing, showing their waked strain, splintering through the limpid soils, muddy waters, merging and merging and merging. Van felt a pang of glory, an ethereal caress of spotlight, courage had an applause when one chose to take the public risk. And here, he raised his knees to stand and one foot, his left, in front, his right, in back, and his shoulders facing left, his arms out sideways, he balanced the windy, wooden waves. He side-stepped and the tree had a divot; and instead of stepping down to it, using his back arm for secu-rity, he skipped over and slid on the lubricated tusk to reach the destined nose. The bent, dying, soaking axis where he stood in Chance's heart culminated with a sun spot, for the great focus light appeared wiping the cloud curtains away, the minimal reveal, and Van's head wore an illumined crown. His spectators roared and walloped in the pleasure of sharing an experience of great danger and gamble and positive payoff.

Van smiled at the expense of Nature and gathered a grand quantity of pride where the pallor had paled his face prior to the prime act of valor. For a showcase opportune for a man in the making to test his abilities in fear's faculties, and to thereby breach the barrier, has an utmost desirous quality. Self-satisfaction. The audience was a bonus, the boy thought, yet would he have known it, that quintessential seizure of time and space to create a moment, a scene, to result had it not been for his friends' encouragements?

It was all their faults that he had gotten thus far, and then, the tree cracked halfway and he toiled in gravity's wake and used an impulse to hang on one branch with his dominant hand. His final task, to toss the firecrackers into the bowl, was a success. At the conclusion, he had sprained an ankle landing in the ford. It was worthwhile and not to be forgotten.

9

In A Line To Get Out

He knew nothing of the station. He did not know that the girl at the ticket booth had come down with a fever and that the police officer was smitten by her and the way she looked on display through the glass pane. He did not know that the second track had been closed because a drunk had been killed stumbling off the edge and crushed not six hours before. He only knew that Her train was running late and he had to wait longer.

He drank his coffee in a plastic cup. The time when there was a diner with cozy warmth and glass mugs was long gone. It did not bother him, for he had gotten used to being alone. Not a feeling of dread called loneliness, just a normal position for the majority of time. The loud speaker blared a steady murmur of protocols that he naturally ignored.

But at the announcement that a Henry Blackman please make his way to the nearest reservation counter, he noticed and proceeded. The day's newspaper and coffee cup stayed where he had sat. He thought he was to return. At the nearest counter, three men and an old lady were ahead of him, so he got in line. The loud speaker repeated itself and he heard his name broadcasted again. It only bothered him because he felt exposed.

When you wait in line, single file, and no one speaks but the one person who has reached the front, you notice your isolation. It is more comforting in a closed space, like a hallway or a bus stop, because there is no place else to look or go. The counter line was not a better place. Late travelers and bodies busy in motion had to alter their routes to avoid the line that had grown behind him to ten people.

A few minutes passed and there was only one man at the counter and the old lady waiting ahead. More than a few minutes passed and the old lady grew annoyed. She shuffled her feet first, then checked her watch more than once, and started to glance back to Henry Blackman. Her gaze had all the searchings of wandering eyes looking for another weary sufferer. Henry Blackman avoided her gaze as best he could. He did not want to be rude so on the third time she looked back, he looked below to meet her and hitched his eyebrows up and down. That was enough recognition for her to leave him alone.

The man started flailing his arms and curling over to emphasize his imperatives. He demanded reference to a manager, anyone in a position of power. The counter attendant looked like he did not belong at such a place. He was a great size too much for the attendant seat and his shoulders stuck out on both sides of the customer of grievance. He shook his head, still showing a sign of respect, but had no answer. If the system was wrong, there was no matter. A double negative. Everything cancelled out.

Defeat was not acceptable for the angry man. He conceded if he had physical proof, a receipt, that contradicted the system, the system should be corrected. And if not, the system should cater to the customer and rectify its error. He had a point.

But the grumblings of the line had doubled and tripled until sputterings of obscenities and a steady murmuring of frustration spilled behind the man, now at his deluded epicenter of a claim. A claim to fight, for what was right, for principle, and desire for a benefit at the outcome.

Henry Blackman could not help but feel for the man. Not so much for the man himself but for his position. It was his right to try to resolve the issue and he had waited in line fair and civil. He also was creating a scene and creating a scene meant a longer time to wait for everyone else. This problem posed to the front of Henry Blackman's mind as the time passed Her train's scheduled arrival. Figuring the delay could not be more than ten minutes, Henry Blackman guessed the man ahead would shy away from the scene because it was just a smarter decision. To give up, unable to win. The system was cold.

Before the angry man made up his mind, the old lady ahead of Henry Blackman had had enough and vanished. The angry man did as Henry Blackman had guessed.

The counter attendant looked glad to be rid of a problem in the form of the angry man and smiled gaily when Henry Blackman approached the counter. The man behind the counter acted as if he was expecting Henry Blackman. He said, oh, yes, and unveiled a document from the fax machine underneath the counter. He read the message aloud. Personal notes were no longer passed along.

She was not coming on the train that pulled in late when Henry Blackman was at the counter. She hadn't a mobile phone or a reason. The man behind the counter felt bad for Henry Blackman. Henry Blackman had heard the message spoken aloud and looked passed the man behind the counter to process the news. All he said was thank you and carried on to an exit where the pale light of the overcast day remained. He left his coffee and paper and another man moved the coffee to the seat next and took the paper to read. Blackman lit a cigarette before he was out of the station and scuffed disgust.

Waiting. Waiting. And nothing.

Milton Keynes UK
Ingram Content Group UK Ltd.
UKHW050056231124
3064UKWH00045B/23